For Arthur, the bravest knight in the kingdom! With love x
~ T. C.

For Cora—my newest cousin (twice removed!)
~ A. E.

tiger tales
5 River Road, Suite 128, Wilton, CT 06897
Published in the United States 2015
Originally published in Great Britain 2015
by Little Tiger Press
Text copyright © 2015 Tracey Corderoy
Illustrations copyright © 2015 Alison Edgson
ISBN-13: 978-1-58925-177-9
ISBN-10: 1-58925-177-6
Printed in China
LTP/1400/0990/0914
All rights reserved
10 9 8 7 6 5 4 3 2 1

For more insight and activities,
visit us at www.tigertalesbooks.com

I Want My Daddy!

by Tracey Corderoy   Illustrated by Alison Edgson

tiger tales

Arthur was having a bad day.
His castle kept tumbling down.
   "Too wibbly," Arthur frowned.
"Too wobbly!"
   He picked up his dragon Huffity
and stomped away. "I want my daddy!"
he grumbled.

"Daddy," groaned Arthur,
"my castle keeps falling down!"
"Oh, dear," said Daddy. "Let's see!"
And he followed his little knight
through the yard.

"Hmmm," Daddy nodded. "This looks like a job for more than *one* knight."

"Are *you* a knight, too, Daddy?" Arthur asked.

"I certainly am!" Daddy smiled. "Knights together?"

"Knights forever!" cried Arthur.

Arthur's daddy found a big pot of glue. "This," he said, "is castle *cement!*"

"Oooo!" gasped Arthur, stepping closer.

He helped Daddy to cement and paint, and make the turrets nice and straight.

"And all castles need a flag," Arthur said, planting one on the top.

"There!" he cried. "We did it! Yippee!"
"Great job!" Daddy chuckled.

While Daddy finished
his own jobs, Arthur played
knights with Huffity.

"Charge!" roared Arthur,
chasing all around his kingdom—
faster, and faster,

He marched and climbed.
He swished his sword.
Then he found a good horse
and galloped off . . . .

until ...

"Ouch," squeaked Arthur,
rubbing his leg. He took a
deep breath and cried,

"Daddy!"

"It's okay, my big brave knight!" said Daddy, rushing over with a hug. "How about we visit your *favorite* castle?"

"The one in the park?" Arthur asked. "That's Huffity's favorite castle, too!"

So off they went together.

"Here we are!" said Daddy.
"Hooray!" Arthur cheered.
The castle had turrets and
ladders and a great big slide!

They marched
around it.

They climbed up . . .

and slid down. And they
talked about kings and
crowns.

"Now let's fish for monsters
in the moat!" cried Arthur.
So they sat side by side,
and waited, and waited . . . .

Then, suddenly something tugged at
Arthur's line.
   "Daddy—a monster!" yelled Arthur.
"I caught one!"
But what if it was big?
And hairy?
And scary!

"Daddy!"

"Here I am!" called Daddy. "I was just getting our snacks."

"But I caught a monster!" Arthur cried. Arthur wasn't scared now that his daddy was there.

So they pulled, and pulled, and pulled, until . . .

Splosh!

Out came
the monster!
"A Boot-a-saurus!" Daddy chuckled.
"A Boot-a-saurus?" giggled Arthur.
And they laughed and laughed
all the way home.

Later, while playing in his castle in the yard, Arthur made a big, sparkly crown. Every knight needed a king for his castle. And Arthur's king needed to be someone very special . . . .

Someone who was
missing him, right now.
"Arthur?" called Daddy.
"Arthur? Where are you?"

"Surprise!"

shouted Arthur, jumping out and
plunking the crown on Daddy's head.
"Hugs together?" Daddy asked.
"Hugs forever!" cheered Arthur.
And he gave his daddy the biggest hug
in the *whole* kingdom!